Credit: H. K. Stuart/Garter Lane Arts Centre

Sarah Bowie is a writer and illustrator from Ireland. In addition, she is an arts educator and runs workshops in schools on comic-making, visual storytelling and doodling for well-being. Sarah also co-founded The Comics Lab as well as Ireland's first Graphic Short Story Prize in partnership with the **Irish Times**. **Nina Peanut is Amazing** is her debut middle-grade novel.

Published in the UK by Scholastic, 2024
1 London Bridge, London, SE1 9BG
Scholastic Ireland, 89E Lagan Road, Dublin Industrial Estate,
Glasnevin, Dublin, D11 HP5F

SCHOLASTIC and associated logos are trademarks and/or
registered trademarks of Scholastic Inc.

Text and illustrations © Sarah Bowie, 2024

The right of Sarah Bowie to be identified as the author and illustrator
of this work has been asserted by them under the Copyright,
Designs and Patents Act 1988.

ISBN 978 0702 3 2987 6

A CIP catalogue record for this book is available from the British Library.

Printed by C&C in China.
Paper made from wood grown in sustainable
forests and other controlled sources.

1 3 5 7 9 10 8 6 4 2

www.scholastic.co.uk

NINA PEANUT IS AMAZING

SARAH BOWIE

SCHOLASTIC

To Liz and Ken
and their chickens

Uh-oh.

NINA! PAY ATTENTION!

Mr Harrison (we call him Mr HAIRYSON — you can guess why)

Uh ... yes, sir!

Anyway, as I was saying ... you've probably seen my channel: it's **HUGE.**

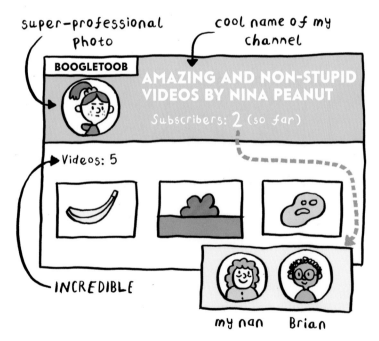

super-professional photo

cool name of my channel

BOOGLETOOB

AMAZING AND NON-STUPID VIDEOS BY NINA PEANUT

Subscribers: 2 (so far)

Videos: 5

INCREDIBLE

my nan   Brian

Someday I will have a **MILLION**
– no, actually, more like a

GAZILLION

followers.

You should SUBSCRIBE

I'm about to say **"Nina"**, which is technically the last thing he said (before he said **"Repeat the last thing I just said"**) when the bell goes. Phew.

That was a lucky escape.

This is
BRIAN.
He is my

MAIN SUBSCRIBER

and also my

BEST
FRIEND

since AGES AGO.

He is also sometimes my
VIDEO-MAKING ASSISTANT
and does things like **holding the camera**
when I have to do **interviews** and stuff.

What's your
favourite —
carrots or
pizza?

Interesting
choice.

"WILL this video be as good as your LAST ONE?"
Megan says.
She's talking about ...

It's actually one of my more
GENIUS IDEAS.

Unfortunately, there's no way for your **EYEBALLS** to avoid seeing one of Megan Dunne's **TOTALLY DULL DOG VIDEOS** if you go to Dozyville Primary School.

Everyone here is **ALWAYS** going on about them ...

... even though they are **SUPER BORING.**

I only make **AMAZING** videos about **SERIOUS** things like:

HOW TO PEEL A BANANA

♥ 2 💬 1

Nanny Peanut: very informative, pumpkin

and:

HOW TO NOT STEP IN POO

♥ 2 💬 1

Brian: wish I'd watched this sooner

See? **TOTALLY INTERESTING!**

11

Oh no, not **POINTY-OUT PAMELA!**
I thought we'd missed her. Pointy-Out Pamela is a
girl on my street who **loves POINTING STUFF OUT**,
especially if it is:

A OBVIOUS
e.g. "It's raining."

B ANNOYING
e.g. "You're going
to be late."

C BORING
e.g. "That bird
is on a
branch."

D INSULTING
e.g. "You smell
like yoghurt."

Mum makes me walk to school with her every morning
(**"She's a very nice girl!"**), but I usually hide in the
toilets after school till she's gone ... except today
because of my

AMAZING VIDEO IDEA!

"Brian," Pointy-Out Pamela says. "**That's a book on science.**" (Pointy-Out Thing No. 1)
"Nina, you've got crisps on your chin." (Pointy-Out Thing No. 2)

"Remember, Brian," I say. "**We have to go to ...**"
(thinking) "**...the SHOE SHOP!**" (not bad) "To buy Nan a ... a ... a ..."

"**EXACTLY!**" I say, relieved.
"**Why just ONE SHOE?**" Brian says.
"You never mentioned this before."

I give Brian the **Secret Eyebrow Code**, which means:
"**This is just to get rid of Pamela.**"

But then I realize I just made this code up,
so Brian has **NO IDEA** what I'm on about.
"**It's for HOPPING, Brian,**" I say. "**Nan LOVES
hopping.**" (I'm still doing the Secret Code.)

Now we have to go the **EXTRA-LONG** way home.

Brian's house

tennis courts

park for football and stuff

Dozyville Primary School

my house

annoying wall

Pamela's house

NOT NORMAL WAY HOME:
For Emergency Situations Only
(15 mins 20 secs)

NORMAL WAY HOME:
(5 mins 45 secs)

That was a bit **MEAN.**

It's better than FIVE MINUTES and FORTY-FIVE SECONDS of Pamela pointing stuff out.

Then Uncle Freddie drives by.

Uncle Freddie leans out of the window and shouts:
"Enjoy the party on Saturday, Nina!"
"Party? What party?" Brian asks.
"No idea," I say. "But Uncle Freddie seems
to think I'm going."

Fifteen minutes and ten seconds later we are almost **FINALLY** at my house ...

... when **NOSY NORMA** (real name Mrs Thompson) and **HUBERT**, her **LIE-DETECTING TERRIER**, suddenly appear.

Nosy Norma is always asking questions, and if you tell a **LIE**, Hubert will **GROWL** at you.
"**Where have YOU been?**" she asks.
"**The SHOE SHOP,**" I say (in case Pointy-Out Pamela can hear).

Straight away:

GRRRRR!

scary

It's only when you tell the **TRUTH** ...

I mean, I PRETENDED to go to the shoe shop!

... that Hubert **WAGS** his **TAIL**.

suddenly friendly

This is how Nosy Norma gets all her **information.**

Just as we get to the front door,
Mum comes rushing out.

There aren't enough **speech** bubbles
for everything on Mum's list.

"C'mon, Brian, lets go and say hi to Nan."
Nan has been doing art since Uncle Freddie got her
a **PAINT-BY-NUMBERS** set for Christmas last year.
Now she says she is a **PROPER ARTIST** because she
doesn't need the **numbers** any more.

Hello, pumpkins.

proper ARTIST'S HAT

proper ARTIST'S STRIPY TOP

proper ARTIST'S MESS everywhere

drives Mum up the wall

Nan is always doing paintings of her friends and family.

Here's one of her **BEST FRIEND, Iris,** who in Real Life has a **NORMAL-SIZED** nose.

Iris hasn't spoken to Nan in **TWO MONTHS.**

This one is of my cousin **Doughnut Declan,** who in Real Life actually **DOES** look a bit like this.

Auntie Sheila (his mum) says that Nan **"OBVIOUSLY needs glasses".**

"I'm working on a NEW PAINTING, pumpkins!" Nan says.

It's of YOUR MUM, Brian!

does NOT look like Brian's mum

Oh ... thanks. I'm sure she'll ... uh ... LOVE it.

Good thing **Hubert** isn't here.

Nan gets so excited. I could **never** tell her that maybe she should go back to using **NUMBERS.**

By the way, this is Grandad Peanut, who was **HEAD TRUMPET TESTER** at the Dozyville Trumpet Factory. He died when I was a baby.

this is a **PHOTO** (**not** a Nan painting)

lips gone **HUGE** from all the **TRUMPETS**

bit of **TRUMPET**

Nan says he couldn't drink a **CUP OF TEA** properly because of his lips ...

SPLASH!

... but he could **KISS** her from the **OTHER** **SIDE** of the room.

OH, YOU!

MWAH!

In the end, to get his lips back to **Almost Normal** size, Grandad invented a **TRUMPET-TESTING MACHINE.**

Now Uncle Freddie uses it to blow up his **BALLOONS.**

This one's for you, Dad.

says this after EVERY balloon

so far that's around **92,635 BALLOONS** in honour of Grandad Peanut

Pumping

My room is very **TOP SECRET**, mostly because Mum gets annoyed whenever she sees it and tells me to **"CLEAN UP AT ONCE!"**

While Brian munches on **CARROT STICKS** ...

Mmm, DELICIOUS.

... I reach for the **BRAIN FOOD***
(not **"BRIAN" FOOD** – that would be disgusting).

in here so Mum won't look

MATHS STUFF

fizzy cola bottles

very powerful brain food

This is something I <u>HAVE</u> to eat, or else my **CREATIVE GENIUS BRAIN** won't work properly. **Look:**

SCIENCE

MY BRAIN

BEFORE brain food

AFTER brain food

Hiiiiiiii!

*Non–Mum–approved

28

Just so you know - this is **LES**.

EYE CRUST (crunchy brown)

EYE GUNK (gooey green)

TAIL (wonky)

MOUTH BREATH

used underpants

+

dead fish

x1,000

BUM BURPS

turkey flavour

Les is about a **HUNDRED** in **human years**. He's been around since way **B.M. (Before Me).**

Me

Here's Les saying "hi" to me when I was still a BUMP.

MEOW!

This is what happens when Les goes to the toilet:

Les's Toilet Tray — untouched

The Floor — touched

Mum's Face

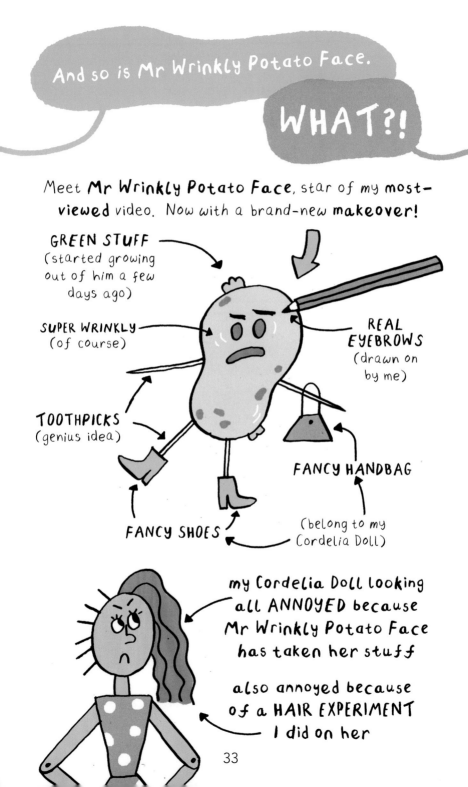

35

37

38

We wait for AGES (twenty-two seconds), but Les just stays there, not moving.

... and WASHING himself.

Much later:

He also smells DUSTBINS.

That's when the phone battery dies.

It's two days since I posted:

A TOTALLY WILD WILDLIFE DOCUMENTARY

So far only Nan has commented:

My brave little pumpkin, making videos even when she's losing her voice.

Love you, Nanny xx

IT'S A TYPICAL DAY

in Dozyville Primary School.

Everyone's going on about
Megan Dunne's latest video ...

... which is FINE if you **LIKE** pony videos.

I just prefer more serious
videos, you know, like
DOCUMENTARIES
and stuff.

46

I stop standing on Brian's foot.

technically true –
Nan _was_ quite
positive

I don't say: still **only two.**

Instead, I blink my eyes
in a **"you are a boring
person"** type of way.

blinking

48

Is MINUS <u>ONE</u> MILLION a number, Ovaltina?

still blinking

Because if it is, THAT'S how many followers Nina Peanut has!

everyone

still blinking (sort of)

HA! HA! HA! HA! HA! HA!

49

"And I want to go to a fashion-show party at Megan's **SO BAD!**" says Amy.

Then she says, "**Sorry.**"

"It's **OK,**" I say **(LIE)**, and give Amy the invitation back.

EVERY girl in the class is invited ...
EXCEPT ME.

Here's me pretending to read a **VERY LARGE BOOK.**

Brian said I could hold SQUIDGE after school today.
He's trying to cheer me up because Megan is
being so **HORRIBLE.**

Squidge is Brian's **hamster**, by the way.

I promise Brian I'll hold Squidge the **PROPER** way this time.

Unfortunately, Brian's big brother, **Jason**, is home.

*What he calls us because of how we catch balls with our NOSES, even when we're trying to use our HANDS.

As usual, we just *ignore* him.

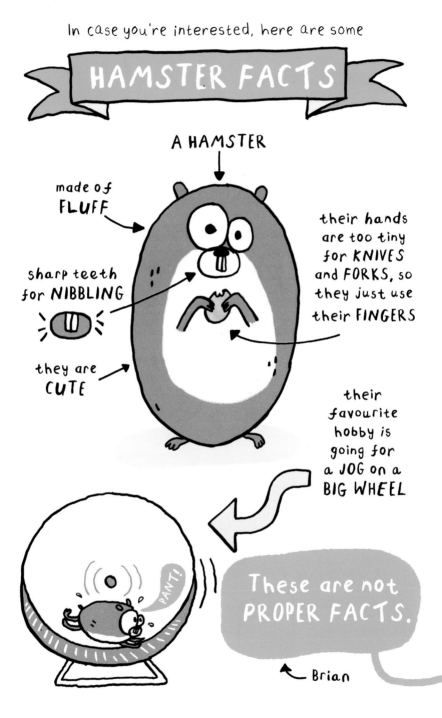

Squidge lives in Brian's bedroom.
Here *is* his house:

SQUIDGE'S HOUSE

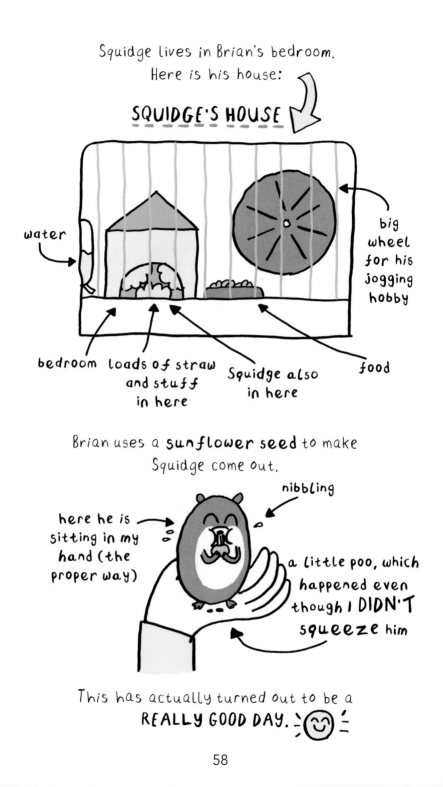

water

big
wheel
for his
jogging
hobby

bedroom   loads of straw
and stuff
in here

Squidge also
in here

food

Brian uses a **sunflower seed** to make
Squidge come out.

nibbling

here he is
sitting in my
hand (the
proper way)

a little poo, which
happened even
though I **DIDN'T**
squeeze him

This has actually turned out to be a
REALLY GOOD DAY.

Megan posted her birthday-party video on Sunday, and even though I told my eyeballs **"NO!"**, they still ended up watching it.

Looks like everyone had **TONS of FUN.**

MONDAY MORNING ...

... is as **ANNOYING** as I **thought** it would be.

what she calls her followers

See? **ANNOYING!**

annoyed

Then Mr Hairyson walks in.

He says he has an **announcement**.

"Class, this year we will have an end-of-term talent show ... with a **TWIST!**"

"Ooh, a **TWIST!**" Naomi Tsang says.

"Is it **DOUGHNUTS?**" Ryan Peterson says.

"**No,**" says Mr Hairyson, looking annoyed.

After ten more minutes of everyone trying to guess what the twist is, Mr Hairyson says: "**PETS! The twist is PETS.**"

Mr Hairyson tells us we can have our **ACTUAL PET** in our act. On the **ACTUAL STAGE.** (Wow!) However, if your pet is ...

(A) TOO BIG
(like Tanya Moore's pet COW, Daisy)

Moo.

Stop looking at me.

or **(B) TOO SCARED OF FAME**
(like Ernie Eilberg's GERBIL, Jennifer)

or **(C) DOESN'T EXIST**
(like Sophie Elison's imaginary GOLDFISH, Gertie)

I'm not even real.

... then you can do your act **ABOUT** your pet, and you don't need to have them in it.

Things get even better when Mr Hairyson says we get to work with a **PARTNER.**

Straight away, me and Brian say:

Partners!

So do Megan and Ovaltina (**copycats**):

Partners!

Me and Brian start coming up with

straight after school.

After only **ONE** fizzy cola bottle:

"Hang on," Brian says. "**What's this got to do with the TALENT SHOW? And what about LES, your ACTUAL PET?**"

"I'm coming to that, Brian. Just listen," I say, and I have some more brain food while I try to think of something. **(Chew.)** Got it.

That's when Mr Wrinkly Potato Face has an **AMAZING IDEA.**

Me and my best friend, LES, will start a BUSINESS.

has more babies now

SNORE!

"**What kind of business?**" asks Brian.

I say, "**What do babies need more than anything?**"

Food?

Actually, it's SLEEP.

"I'm pretty sure it's **FOOD**," Brian says.
"**No. It's SLEEP,**" I say.

"I still don't understand the business," Brian says.

"It's a BABY-POTATO SLEEPING BUSINESS!"
I say, trying not to roll my eyeballs too much.

"And that's your idea for the talent show?"
Brian says. "Yes," I say, super proud.

won't be as good as mine

"And he'll do normal things like watch a movie and ring his nan."

THE NEXT DAY

at school, Brian is all grumpy.
"Why can't we do both our ideas?" he says.

I just say:

I think it's for the BEST, Brian.

and not
"Your idea is Complete Rubbish" because I'm a **good friend.**

Then Mr Hairyson walks in and says:
"Kids, I forgot to mention, there's another twist." Everyone goes: **"GASP!"**

"YOU don't get to pick your partners." He does an Evil Smile. **"I DO! In fact, I already have."**

We all gasp even more, and then he tells us to check the list on the class noticeboard.

Megan pushes her way through first ...

MOVE.

... and then a second later ...

THE LIST

... she **PRETEND FAINTS.**

"That was a bit strange," Brian says.
"Yeah," I say. "Very."

Eventually, me and Brian make it to the list. Brian spots his name first. **"I'm with Ovaltina,"** he says.

NEXT MORNING

This is me ...

real rain cloud

... and this is Brian ...
all NORMAL and NOT-TRAUMATIZED

Just as I am thinking how **HORRIBLE** my **LIFE** is,
Megan shows up right in front of my face.
Her eyes are all **PUFFY** as if she's been crying the
WHOLE NIGHT (insulting).

I don't know why <u>YOU'RE</u> looking upset.

shocked

This is like **WINNING** the **LOTTO** for you.

MEGAN'S MANSION

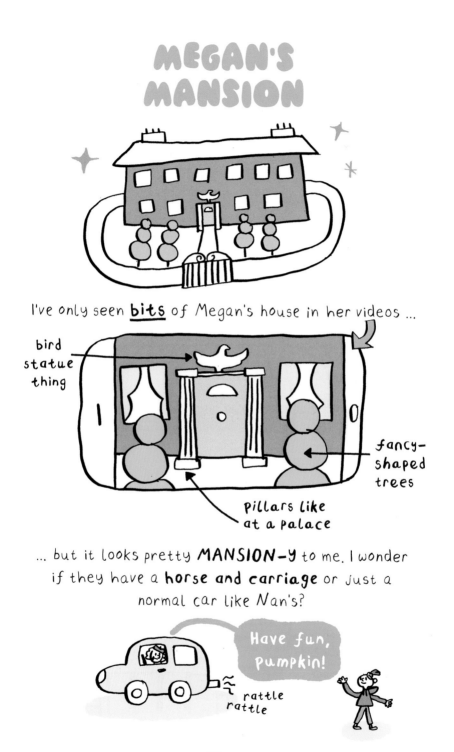

I've only seen **bits** of Megan's house in her videos ...

bird statue thing

fancy-shaped trees

pillars like at a palace

... but it looks pretty **MANSION-y** to me. I wonder if they have a **horse and carriage** or just a normal car like Nan's?

Have fun, pumpkin!

rattle rattle

Before I even get past the gate, I realize that Megan's house is:

JUST ORDINARY.

Megan's house → ← NOT a mansion!

The only thing that makes it a **TINY BIT** mansion-y is all the **FANCY STUFF** around it ...

... like these **statues** on the gate.

quite **MANSION-y**

And this doorbell, which plays a **TUNE:**

doo-dee-doo-dee-dah

very mansion-y

Thankfully, Megan's mum is **NOTHING** like Megan.
She asks me if I'd like a **SNACK** before we get started.

75

She hands me the most **AMAZING** snack box **EVER.**

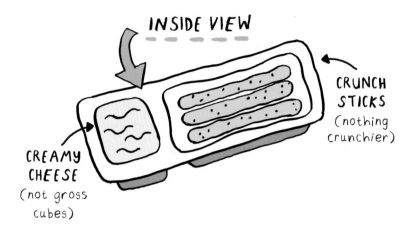

INSIDE VIEW

CRUNCH STICKS (nothing crunchier)

CREAMY CHEESE (not gross cubes)

I can't believe my luck — Mum **NEVER** buys these. I start **MUNCHING** straight away. After a second, I realize that Megan is just sitting there **WATCHING** me, so I try to be polite and ask her when the Dance Instructor is coming. That's when I accidentally **SPIT** some crunch stick right in her eyeball.

MEGAN'S EYEBALL

ew

crunch stick from my mouth (also 'ew')

I have to go and **WASH** my **EYE** now!

"Oh, don't mind Megan," Mira says. "She's very sensitive. Let's wait for her in the garden."

Outside, Mira starts going on about her **GERANIUMS** ...

— who cares?

... but I can't take my eyes off what looks like an

INFLATABLE POOL!

you could pop it with a pin!

So **THIS** is the **HUGE POOL** from Megan's video?

Princess must have been going round in circles!

Next thing, I hear a voice behind me say,
"**Guess what!**" and I turn round to see that Megan
has not only washed her eyeball but she has
also got changed into an
EXTREMELY SPARKLY OUTFIT.

I'M your Dance Instructor.

what?!

sparkly TIARA

sparkly DRESS

sparkly LEGS

sparkly SHOES

"**Hurry up and follow me,**" she says, walking
extremely quickly. I can hardly keep up because of all
the **SHOCK**. A second later, we come to a door at the
end of her hall with this **SIGN** over it:

MEGAN'S DANCE STUDIO

flashing lights

INSIDE VIEW

HUGE mirror

wall full of trophies

another HUGE mirror

I think this is the **FANCIEST** dance studio I've ever seen. (It's also the only one.) Suddenly Megan does a little whistle, and Princess Trixie Bell — who I thought was another **DOG STATUE** — comes running over. She is also wearing a **SPARKLY** outfit.

sparkly **SCRUNCHIES**

grumpy face like Megan's

sparkly **COLLAR**

sparkly **CAPE**

... then starts **DANCING.**

Next, Megan gets a **HOOP** ...	... does another little whistle ...

... and holds it in the air while Princess flies up like a **SUPERHERO** ...

actual **FLYING**

... and goes **STRAIGHT THROUGH** the hoop.

very, very good

Now I see why Megan has all those **TROPHIES.**

A voice behind us says:

Good work, CHAMP!

Megan's dad — must have been WATCHING the whole time

HUGE whistle

A little SLOPPY on the Reverse Hoop Jumps, though.

Yes, Dad.

Remember, we're IN IT ...

... to WIN IT!!

After Megan's dad is gone, I ask her if he's a Dance Instructor too.

"No," she says. "He coaches FOOTBALL."

"Right," Megan says. "It's **YOUR TURN** now."
(Uh-oh.) "Start with **SPINNING** — even **YOU**
can't mess that up." (Gulp.)

I start off pretty slowly, but Megan keeps shouting

FASTER!   FASTER!   until I have gone

TOTALLY BLURRY. This is reminding me of the
TEA CUPS RIDE
at DOZYVILLE FUNFAIR!

SURVIVOR

The next day at school, everyone is talking about Megan's video of me accidentally **SPIN-KICKING** Princess Trixie Bell. She is calling Princess a **SURVIVOR** and says I did it **ON PURPOSE** because I am **JEALOUS** of her **AMAZING TALENT**.

And now Princess has to wear a **BANDAGE** for a **WHOLE WEEK**.

NOT TRUE! Megan **MADE** her mum put a bandage on, even though her mum said:

There's **NOTHING** wrong with her, love. She just had a **FRIGHT**.

See? **HAPPY**

There are **TONS** of comments under the video.
Most of them are about **ME**.

Don't mind her. She is DEFINITELY JEALOUS.

Such a BAD SPINNER!

Poor you, she's a NIGHTMARE!

Brian is about the only person **NOT** giving me dirty looks today. I ask him how it's going with Ovaltina. **"Pretty good,"** he says.

Really?

Yeah, she's actually very nice once you get to know her.

I wish I had a **NOT-HORRIBLE** person for a partner too.

ACCIDENT

Megan's mum had an accident with some new lotions she was making for the Poochie Parlour last night ...

KABOOM!

house full of DOG SHAMPOO

... and now Megan has to come to **MINE** for rehearsals this evening. Yay...

Let's get this OVER WITH.

what's going on here?

not again

bandage on a DIFFERENT LEG

"**Uh ... nice handbag,**" I say, even though I **don't** mean it. "**I know,**" Megan says. "**It's DESIGNER.**" (Show-off.)

Nan comes running out and says:

You must be Megan!

very friendly

Yeah.

very grumpy

She insists on showing Megan her "GALLERY".

"This one's my cousin Norbert and this one is..."
It goes on for AGES.
Eventually: "And THIS one is Nina!"

It really looks like her, Mrs Peanut!

suddenly HOT in here

90

"I'll do one of **YOU** next," Nan says.

"**Uh, thanks, Nan. We have** to go now," I say, and get out of the room fast before she can say anything else.

Your nan's **PAINTINGS** are almost as good as your **DANCING.**

GRRR

Even though I put all the junk from my floor into a box before Megan came, it doesn't stop her from giving my whole room a **DIRTY LOOK** the second she walks in.

STUFF

She gives Les an **ESPECIALLY BIG** dirty look.

asleep on my bed

BUM BURPS not helping

"What is he, like, a HUNDRED?!" Megan says,
holding her nose.

"Yeah, something like that," I say as I pull out
Mr Wrinkly Potato Face. I've had enough of Megan's
HOOPS. It's time she saw my
CREATIVE VISION.

I try to explain about the sleeping business, but
Megan seems confused.

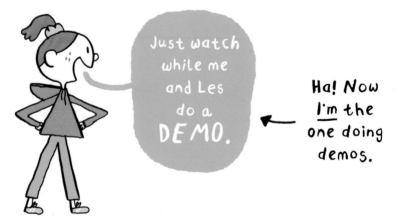

After a second, Megan says:

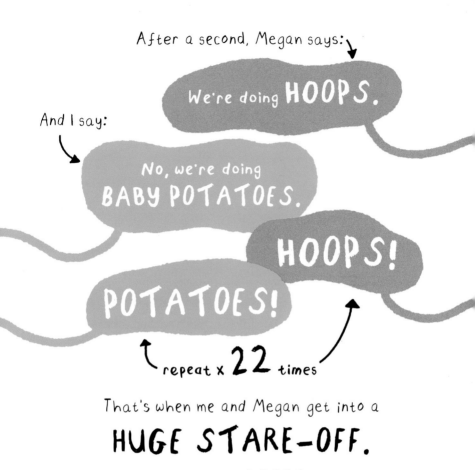

That's when me and Megan get into a

HUGE STARE-OFF.

"First one who blinks LOSES," says Megan.

Eight and a half minutes later:

Huh?

Oh, Les! FOODIES!

Uh-oh.

Nan is doing the **FOODIES SONG.**

Les **LOVES** the Foodies Song.

What was **THAT?!**

I can't look because I'm **STILL** in a **STARE-OFF.**

Here's mine and Megan's eyeballs side by side:

STARE

STARE

Les *is* making even **more** noise now ...

CRASH!

BANG!

... and Megan's eyeballs start to move. Then she looks away, which means –

"**Hey!**" she shouts, and grabs her phone.

I've got to get this on CAMERA!

I finally do a **BIG BLINK** ...

takes ages, eyeballs gone all **STICKY**

... and see Les running around with my

UNDERPANTS

on his **HEAD!**

The more Nan goes **FOODIES,** the more Les crashes into stuff like the wall, the table and

MY LEG →

Finally, Les makes it out of the door ...

... followed by Megan and Princess Trixie Bell.

In the kitchen, Nan says:

There you are, Les!

I was beginning to worry.

She doesn't say anything about the UNDERPANTS!

"Look, it's your FAVOURITE."

BLUNKY CHUNKS

DEAD FISH FLAVOUR

LES

Les has very FUSSY TASTE when it comes to food. He only eats the CHEAP STUFF.

Yum!

"Enjoy!" says Nan, and she rushes back to her painting. (She's started one of Megan.) Les manages to eat **ALL** his food with my **UNDERPANTS** _still_ on his head.

SLURP!

Well, I have EVERYTHING I need for tonight.

LICK

Later:

At school the next day, everyone just IGNORES me the NORMAL amount (phew). This means either videos of cats in underpants are actually TOO BORING to watch (fingers crossed) or Megan just hasn't posted it yet.

Maybe she FORGOT?

Megan with amnesia

WHO am I?

WHY am I here?

But when I get home, I see this:

The Poochie Princess

DON'T MISS OUT!
XTRA SPECIAL
NEW VIDEO!!!
This Sunday @ 6 p.m.

AT LEAST

I'm going to my dad's for the weekend ...

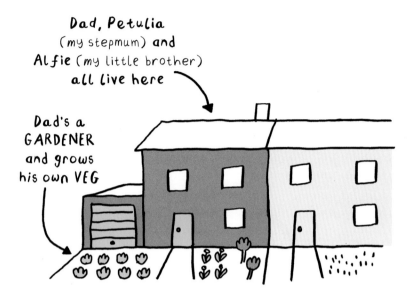

Dad, Petulia (my stepmum) and Alfie (my little brother) all live here

Dad's a GARDENER and grows his own VEG

... because trying to **AVOID** Alfie's **LEG HUGS** will be a good way of keeping my mind **OFF** the video.

This is what happens the **SECOND** I walk in the door.

me just trying to **SURVIVE**

Alfie doing a MASSIVE LEG HUG

Technically, Alfie looks quite cute, but **CLOSE-UP** he *is* FULL of

age 3

NOSE BOGEYS

and

MUSHY BANANA.

Dad and Petulia are always saying "**Ooh, he LOVES his big sister!**" but they're not the ones with Alfie's "*STUFF*" all over their **LEG** (it's *ME!*).

To make things even **MORE GROSS**, Dad is always getting me to eat **GREEN THINGS** that look **EXACTLY** like Alfie's **NOSE BOGEYS**.

It's your FAVOURITE.

NO!!

peas & broccoli (& BOGEYS – obviously)

At least Petulia does **NICE CAKES** (except for the time she made a **GREEN** one).

Not thinking about the video becomes **EVEN EASIER** when Dad takes us to the park on Saturday and Alfie drops his entire **ICE-CREAM CONE** on my trainer.

melt

AAAAAH!

LOUD

waiting for ice cream

MORE melt

definitely **NOT** thinking about the video now

When we get back, Petulia lets me use her laptop to video-call Brian while Dad cleans my shoe.

Hey, Nina!

I start to tell Brian about the **ICE CREAM** (which is actually a pretty cool story), when suddenly his **head** disappears.

There are also **STRANGE NOISES.**

SSSHEEW!

Brian, what's going on?

Sorry, Nina, me and Ovaltina are working on our act.

Ovaltina?

A second later, both heads disappear
again, and I can hear loads of cutting
and tearing sounds.

"OK, then," I say. "See you on
Monday, I suppose."

SUNDAY EVENING @ 6 P.M.

I don't know if the video has been posted yet (too scared to check), but posing for another Nan painting ...

Can you hold the **PINEAPPLE** a little **HIGHER,** pumpkin?

quite **HARD,** actually

... is a good way of avoiding anything to do with *CATS IN UNDERPANTS*. I'm trying not to think about school tomorrow.

MONDAY MORNING

I am expecting **THE WORST** at school today:
pointing, laughing and everyone calling me
"THE UNDERPANTS GIRL".

Instead, the first thing that happens is:

Followed by:

And:

What is **GOING ON?!**

That's what I thought.
Then why is everyone **ACTING FRIENDLY?**

Everyone, that is,
EXCEPT Megan.

She is giving me
EXTRA-DIRTY LOOKS
this morning. I thought
she would be **happy** now
the **WORLD** has seen my
UNDERPANTS.

Unless she really **DOES** have amnesia and
forgot to post the video? I'll have to wait till I
get home to check (no phones at school and Brian
hasn't been on BoogleToob either).

Awesome
video, Nina!

That
little guy
is **SUPER
FUNNY.**

Nope, **NOT** amnesia.

As soon as I get home, I watch the video.

Here's what she wrote:

"Guess who makes her CAT wear her SMELLY UNDERPANTS all day long! Yep, @NinaPeanut101."

Ugh! Trying to make me look bad!

But, hey, look at the COMMENTS!

This is the cutest CAT EVER!!!

Those underpants are very nice. I like them.

This cat's running is AMAZING for a cat that has PANTS on his head!

They're GOOD!

That's when I check my own channel and realize I have

585 NEW FOLLOWERS!

Mum's computer

cannot believe my eyeballs

Tuesday was another good day (621 new followers), but Wednesday was **AMAZING.** That's when **REALLY COOL JOOLS** — who's thirteen and the coolest vlogger ever — tagged me in her video.

Then, guess what. Really Cool Jools **FOLLOWED** me!

By the way, this is **NOT** a dream. In fact, it is
REAL LIFE.

Did you see that REALLY COOL JOOLS followed NINA?

SO AMAZING!

I KNOW!!

me being ALL FAMOUS and STUFF

Guess who Really Cool Jools **DIDN'T** follow.

After school, Pointy-Out Pamela says the
first **NON-ANNOYING** Pointy-Out Thing **EVER.**

I even let Pamela walk home with us for about the
FIRST time in a **hundred years.**

She's really not that bad.

By the way, here's a DIAGRAM of how many FOLLOWERS me and Megan have since last Friday:

THE INVITATION

A *weird* thing happened at school today.

Mum says I have to invite you to THE POOCHIE PARLOUR.

shocked (and hungry)

"And you *have* to bring your DISGUSTING CAT."
All I can think of to say is: "Huh?"

"I know, it's a TERRIBLE idea," Megan says, "but Mum thinks he's CUTE."

me and Brian just LOOKING at each other

"What are you **WAITING** for?" Megan asks.
"Your **SMELLY CAT** is going to get a
FREE MAKEOVER!"

You should be **GRATEFUL.**

I've kind of always wanted to see inside the Poochie Parlour. **"OK,"** I say. **"Good,"** Megan says.

Be there Saturday at ten.

And be **STYLISH.** Mum has **VERY HIGH** standards.

Me and Brian hardly say anything for the rest of lunch.

THE POOCHIE PARLOUR

I tried squeezing Les into Mum's **FANCY GOING-OUT BAG,** but it was **too small.**

only fits one **LES LEG**

So then I had the Creative Genius idea of taking him in **NAN'S SHOPPING TROLLEY.**

full of **TOILET ROLL** in case he has an **"ACCIDENT"**

mostly **CAT**

mostly **TOILET ROLL**

It's actually very **nice** of Megan's mum to invite me.

The POOCHIE PARLOUR

gulp

OPEN

When I go inside, I see **FANCY DOGS** everywhere ...

... getting **STYLISH** things done.

BLOW SNIP BRUSH PAINT

Megan **wasn't** exaggerating.

As soon as she sees me, Megan starts eyeballing Nan's shopping trolley.

Is that DESIGNER?

Yes.

↑
Lie

"Nina!" Megan's mum comes running over.
"This must be DES!"
"Les."

Mira picks him up and gives him a **BIG HUG,** which makes a **BUM BURP** come out, right in Megan's *face.*

He's ADORABLE!

cough

squeeze

stuck

DEAD FISH FLAVOUR

"What shall we start with?" Mira says, putting Les in a Poochifying Pod. "Here, Mum," says Megan, handing her a bottle of dry shampoo. "Thanks, love," says Mira. "How thoughtful!"

No problem, Mum.

suddenly all NICE and SMILEY

"Got your camera ready?" Mira says in a Loud Whisper to Megan. "It's just a couple of pics for our social media," she says to me. "That OK?" "Uh ... I suppose so," I say. Is that the Real Reason she asked me here? To get pictures of Les?

Mira sprays the shampoo all over Les and within HALF a SECOND he starts to have an
EXTREME REACTION:

eye gunk

bogey

extra mouth breath

bits of dry shampoo

bum burps

Finally, after **AGES** of sneezing, Les stops. That's when we realize we are all covered in his **eye gunk** and **nose bogeys**:

Meanwhile, Les looks ...

... AMAZING

tail less wonky

eye gunk all gone

no more bogeys

bum all empty

fur extra fluffy

"That's never happened before," Mira says, looking at the shampoo bottle. "Hmm, it's not one of my USUAL ones."

While Mira and Megan are cleaning themselves **(ew)**, I take a closer look at the bottle.

like an ACTUAL DETECTIVE

129

The label starts to **PEEL OFF** ...

... and underneath is the **REAL** one.

SNEEZING POWDER

This is extremely **DASTARDLY.** Even for Megan.
"I have to say," Mira says, "this new shampoo
is **VERY IMPRESSIVE.** Take some more
photos, love."

missed a bit

They'll look **GREAT** on the website!

Megan says she's going to post her video of Les tonight. She says she's got CLOSE-UPS of his Big Green Bogeys flying everywhere.

It's VERY DISTURBING to watch, actually.

"No one's going to LIKE him once they've seen how GROSS he is," she says.

This is TYPICAL. Just as I was beginning to get REALLY FAMOUS.

SNIFF.

MONDAY MORNING (AGAIN!)

Wondering how the kids at school will react to Megan's video is becoming quite **STRESSFUL.**

Not again.

mouth gone all **TREMBLY**

When I get in, I see a **CROWD** around my desk.

all wearing **CAT EARS**

Brian can't get to his seat

As soon as they see me, they start shouting

WE LOVE LES!

Does this mean they **DIDN'T MIND** his sneezing?

Meanwhile, Megan is at the back of the class being **ALL QUIET** like she's thinking up **ANOTHER DASTARDLY PLAN.**

133

Later in the canteen, suddenly out of nowhere:

Hiiiiiii!

super friendly

completely ignoring Brian

big chew

"I've been thinking," Megan says. "Seeing as you and me are PARTNERS and all, we should hang out more."

still chewing

Just YOU and ME!

EXTRA smiley

"And Princess and LES, of course!"
I look over at Brian, expecting him to be almost CHOKING on his chicken salad, but instead of paying attention to me ...

... he and Ovaltina are **GIGGLING**.

"How about **TONIGHT?**" she says.
"I dunno, Megan, I—"

"OK," I say. "**I'll check with Mum.**"

THE SLEEPOVER

Mum says I can stay at Megan's, as long as I remember to brush my teeth.

It's nice to see you making some NEW FRIENDS...

This time, when I ring Megan's fancy doorbell ...

dum-diddy-dum

different tune

... she seems **GLAD** to see me.

NINA!!!

proper cat basket thing

My main thought is:

What is her
DASTARDLY PLAN
and **WHEN** will it happen?

First, we grab two **SNACK BOXES each** from the kitchen ("**Mum said we could**") and then go up to Megan's bedroom, which in her videos looks all perfect and princessy:

After the shock of her Big Mansion and Huge Pool, I'm not expecting much in **Real Life**, though. Oh wait, it **IS** all **PERFECT** and **PRINCESSY**.

← what?!

Almost. Then I notice **TONS OF MESS**
all over the floor...

Middle bit:
all perfect

Outside bit:
full of SMELLY SOCKS
& Cordelia dolls with NO
CLOTHES on

"Oh, it's OK," she says
when she sees me eyeballing
the slice of toast with a
MUSHROOM growing on it.
"As long as it doesn't
show up in the video, it's **FINE.**"

We sit on her bed and start munching
on our snack boxes.

drooling

snoring

ZZZZZZZ

Just as I'm crunching the crunchiest crunch stick ever, Megan says: **"I'm sorry about the POTATOES."**

"Hey, I have an IDEA!" she says.

Let's make a VIDEO!

"A video?" I say. "About what?"
"About US and our SUPER-COOL PETS!"
Why would Megan want to do a video with me?
It's not like we have to do one for the talent show.
"C'mon, it'll be fun," she says, then sticks her
hands into a huge pile of clothes and pulls out:

TA-DA!

a FANCY
camera
stand

"Just one more thing," she says, and grabs a
tiara from her Tiara Shelf.

very Megan

She asks me if I want one, and I say: **"NO!"**
"Suit yourself," she says, and hits "record".

BESTIE?! That's taking things a bit far!
Does Ovaltina know?

It was actually ME who made him famous in the first place, you know.

HUH?!

If I hadn't posted that video, then Really Cool Jools (who I LOVE, by the way!) would never even have HEARD of Nina or her cat.

Or her UNDERPANTS.

HEY!

me giving Megan a SUPER-HUGE DIRTY LOOK

Anyway, Poochies, back to TODAY'S video!

We're going to demo some AMAZING tricks with our very CUTE PETS!

"Let's start with Princess Trixie Bell."

Princess, walk like a PERSON!

straight away Princess does THIS the SAME as a person

Now pretend you're a FAIRY!

FLAP

very FAIRY-ISH

nearly FLYING

After a few more tricks (including Princess drinking a pretend cup of tea), Megan throws her a doggy biscuit.

Good girl!

Then Megan turns to me and says: "**your turn.**" At first, Les is even **MORE ASLEEP** than before, but then he smells Princess's treat and he is **SUDDENLY AWAKE.**

smell of doggy biscuit

"**Does he do any tricks?**" Megan asks. "**Um ... kind of.**" I put Les on my shoulders and say:

This is Les being a **SCARF.**

fashion

"**Is that it?**" Megan says.
"**I think so.**" She doesn't look very impressed.
I should've brought Mr Wrinkly Potato Face.

Megan turns back to the camera and says:

Well, my Poochies, that's it for today.

But join us again SOON for MORE Princess and Les CUTENESS!

MORE Princess and Les?

BYEEEEEE!!!

whisper

WAVE!

She wants this to happen AGAIN?! WHY?!

me waving

Megan hits "Stop Recording", then says **"Oh!"** when she sees the time. **"I almost forgot — I need to go and film Lorenzo."**

I ask if I can come too, but Megan says, **"No."**

Which is a pity, because I'd **LOVE** to pet a pony's nose.

When she gets back, Megan says:

By the way, you can post our video to **YOUR CHANNEL** too if you like.

That way we **BOTH** get **MORE FOLLOWERS.**

Is **THIS** Megan's Dastardly Plan?

The SLEEP part of the sleepover

To get **MORE FAME?**
Which means me and Les would get **MORE FAME** too?

MORE FAME!!

Woo-hoo!

THE NEXT DAY

at school, I tell Brian about the **PRETTY COOL** video me and Megan just made.

> That's the first time I've ever heard you *call* one of **MEGAN'S VIDEOS** "cool".

"**That's because it's the first time I'M in one,**" I say, and to be honest, I think Brian could have a more **POSITIVE ATTITUDE** about it.

I almost don't want to tell him that Nan has made his **FAVOURITE** Special Pudding for later.

custard and mushy banana

EW!

But I do anyway.

Oh sorry, I totally FORGOT to tell you...

I'm going to OVALTINA'S after school today.

But you ALWAYS come to MINE on a Tuesday!

"Sorry, me and Ovaltina **have** to work on our **ACT**." Again? That's almost **EVERY DAY** for a week Brian's been seeing Ovaltina. What's really going on? And why was Brian's face **ALL RED** that time he was talking to her in the canteen?

That's when I have a very

HORRIBLE THOUGHT...

WHAT IF BRIAN AND OVALTINA ARE IN LOVE?

BLAW!

I need to remember how many times I've seen them:

A Looking into each other's **EYES** for **AGES.**

ICK!

B Talking only to each other and **NO ONE** else.

Blah! Blah!

no one

C Laughing at each other's **STUPID JOKES.**

Ha ha ha!

Ha!

Oh, ha ha **HA!**

And most **SERIOUSLY** of all:

D **SMILING** at each other for **NO REASON.**

EW!

The problem is, I've been **TOO BUSY** being **FAMOUS** to really notice. But from now on, I'm going to be

PAYING ATTENTION.

me paying ATTENTION

Megan's in a **GOOD MOOD** today.

Hey, Bestie!

↑
LOUD

looks a bit HURT

We both posted our video yesterday and got **LOADS** of likes and follows.

FOLLOWER UPDATE

ME

MEGAN

68,320

31,428

Still MORE!

Most of the comments are about **Les:**

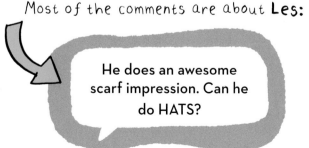

He does an awesome scarf impression. Can he do HATS?

A Les fan from
school even made a
LES PLUSHIE!

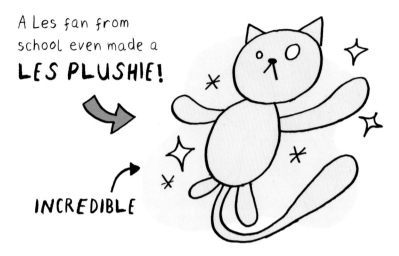

INCREDIBLE

Megan doesn't seem to mind that I'm the most
FAMOUS one, and says we should do another
VIDEO COLLAB soon.

Why don't you
come to MINE
tomorrow?

We can
work on our
ACT too.

Tomorrow? That sounds a bit **TOO SOON** to me.

Before I can answer, my **eyes** get **distracted** by

DEFINITELY IN LOVE!

"Nina, are you **LISTENING** to me?" Megan says.

Nan makes me take **THIS** when I go round to Megan's.

me
waiting at
Megan's
door

Nan's
portrait
of Megan

pretty
BAD
(even
by Nan's
standards)

"It'll put a **smile on her face**," Nan says.
I bet it **WON'T.**

Here's Megan's **ACTUAL FACE** when she sees it:

What's
THAT
meant
to be?

you?

"**Actually, I've got a surprise for you too! Follow me,**" she says, and throws Nan's painting behind her dad's **GOLF CLUBS.**

Up in her room, Megan hands me this:

a **TYPICAL** Megan T-shirt

"It's for you," she says.
"It'll look good in our videos."

Go on, put it on.

A few seconds later:

this is **DEFINITELY** more **LOVE HEART-y** than what I'd normally go for!

"It looks **amazing!**" Megan says, all happy. I don't know why but I feel a bit **SICK** on the inside.

Downstairs in the kitchen, Megan says, **"I've got some SPECIAL TREATS for us,"** and puts two **TINY CUPS** on the table.

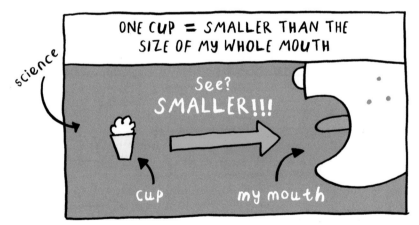

"That won't last me very long," I say. Megan starts laughing. **"Don't be silly,"** she says. **"We'll be having THESE!"** She brings over two **NORMAL-SIZE** cups of hot chocolate.

"So who are the tiny cups for?" I ask.
"They're for Princess and Les, of course," she says.

"Haven't you ever seen

POOCHUCCINOS

before?"

Uh, no I haven't. Megan says they're just cups of whipped cream. "Princess **ADORES** them."

obviously →

prefers Blunky Chunks

SLURP

LICK

Les ends up with most of it on his **FACE.**

AMAZING.

← Megan →

160

Les's bum burps are **EXTRA STINKY** on the drive home from Megan's.

SOUR CREAM flavour

wearing my NORMAL clothes again

Nan says: "**By the way ...**"

... Brian called for you earlier.

really?!

"I told him you were making another video with that lovely girl Mildred." (Lovely girl?!)
"He looked so disappointed. I gave him an extra-big bowl of my Special Pudding to take home."
(Ew.)

"Nan, stop the car," I say as we pass Brian's house.
"I'm going in." "To Brian's? OK, pumpkin, I'll wait
till you give me a wave."

At the door, Mr Babalola says:

"I'll tell him you were here," he calls as I walk
back to the car.

"Not in? That's a shame," Nan says. "Now tell
me again about those **cappuccinos for dogs.**"

There are LOADS of comments on our latest video.

163

Next day during lunch break, Brian keeps going on about some *weird* food called **"CHURROS"** that Ovaltina's Spanish nanny made yesterday evening.

"Pretty good, actually," I say. "Poochuccinos
are really very DELICIOUS, you know."
"If you're a DOG," Brian says, laughing.

By the way, rehearsals for the talent show are going **NOT AMAZING.** Megan is being a Big Bossy-Face again, telling me and Les what to do the whole time. Mostly Les just **IGNORES** her ...

... so I have to walk around with a cat treat tied to a fishing rod just to get him to do

BASIC MOVEMENTS.

I've tried reminding Megan about my
CREATIVE VISION

but she just says: "Oh, yeah, soon."
Then yesterday she said: "You know what
this act needs?"

More
TIARAS!

Oh no,
not...

... MEGAN'S MAGIC
NOSE-BOGEY TIARA

EW!

The one Megan wore for **No Uniform Day** last year
(**typical**) and that me and Brian made a
GENIUS COMIC about...

Soon Megan's **GIANT NOSE BOGEYS** are all over this guy.

If I wear this, Brian will think I've completely

SOLD OUT.

Nina, I really think you're OVER-REACTING.

It will be good for the act, and it will look AMAZING in our videos.

Then Megan says: "**Our followers will love it. And be honest, have I been wrong yet?**"
She has a point.

By the way ...

... you should also wear THIS.

"**What are you wearing?**" Megan says when she opens the door. She looks really worried. I just walk straight past her and into the dance studio ...

... where I reveal the most **SPARKLY OUTFIT** ever invented.

keeping sunglasses on to protect **EYEBALLS** from all the **SPARKLES**

the NOSE-BOGEY TIARA (of course)

FRECKLES, NOT sparkles

NORMAL trainers

YAY!

Megan is so happy it's **ANNOYING.**

literally jumping for joy

"We're SO going to **WIN** now!" she says, then straight away switches into being a **Bossy-Face** again.

BOOP!

Get moving with that **FISHING ROD!**

174

I start off doing all my usual stuff like ...

WALKING the cat

Les, jump.

I said JUMP!

HOLDING a hoop

Lick

trying not to FALL OVER

wobble

... except this time I keep sneaking **TINY LOOKS** at myself in the mirror ...

PEEP!

... and I can't help but notice ...

... I LOOK FABULOUS IN SPARKLES!

Which is surprising because I thought sparkles were just for **GIRLY GIRLS** like Megan and not *Creative Genius* types like **ME.**

Before I know it, the sparkles are taking over my body and making me do this **AMAZING DANCE:**

wow, look at my **LEG!**

almost a **HANDSTAND**

the most **SPLITS** I have EVER done!

I keep going for ages. I never knew I was such a **good dancer!**

Megan must be worried she's got **COMPETITION** now
I know about the **Power of the Sparkles.**

She runs off to feed Lorenzo, and I start looking at her **BORING PHOTOS** for something to do.
They're mostly of her winning trophies.

YAWN!

Then:

WHOOPS!

Hey, there's **ANOTHER** photo underneath!

some girls on
PONIES

Megan just on her
LEGS with NO pony

Next thing, Mira walks in with some **snacks.**

ugh, HEALTHY

This must be from before Megan got Lorenzo.

Is that what Megan's doing now? FEEDING LORENZO?

"Yep," I say.

"Oh dear, I thought we'd finished with all that," she says, and rushes off looking worried.

still EW

Why doesn't Megan's mum want her feeding Lorenzo any more?

Megan posted this video today:

MORE BEHIND-THE-SCENES AT REHEARSALS

♥ 64k 💬 1,284

Hey, she took my Sparkle Dance out! I knew she was JEALOUS! She was right about my outfit, though. Everyone seems to really like it!

Loving the SPARKLES, Nina!

Awesome TIARA!

You two make such a CUTE team!

But WHAT will BRIAN think?

At school the next day, I can hardly look Brian in the eye when I say "Hi" (too embarrassed).

Since when did you and Ovaltina get GLUED TOGETHER like ...

... two things that are GLUED TOGETHER?

Huh?

"You and Ovaltina," I say. "You're always hanging out."

"What about you and Megan?" Brian says. "You're always at her house making videos."

"I only did the Poochuccino one because you and Ovaltina were being all DISGUSTING and IN LOVE in the canteen." "What?! In love? No way!" he says. "We're just friends." (Yeah, right!)

"Then why are you always laughing at her stupid jokes?" I say.

And STARING into her EYES for NO REASON?

Then he says: "**Now all you're interested in is getting FAMOUS with Megan. You're even starting to ACT like her.**"

"**Then how do you explain that love-heart T-shirt and the nose-bogey tiara?**" Brian says.

He's right. It does look like I'm copying her.

"**Well, maybe I wouldn't have to spend so much time with Megan,**" I say ...

Everybody's head spins round, including Ovaltina's.
Brian's face is completely red like an **UNUSUALLY
LARGE STRAWBERRY.**

"**Very good, Nina,**" Mr Hairyson says. "**I look
forward to seeing your HOMEWORK.**"

Me and Brian don't say another word to each other the **WHOLE** morning. At lunch, we walk to the canteen in **TOTAL SILENCE,** like we're stuck inside a **VIDEO** with the mute button on...

no subtitles   not even any lips to read   AWKWARD

Then, just as we get to the canteen, Brian starts to say something ...

Nina, I—

lunch bag

... when Megan comes running up and throws her arms around my neck.

"See? I told you people would **LOVE** the **TIARA**," Megan says. "**Uh, yeah,**" I say, trying not to sound **TOO ENTHUSIASTIC** in front of Brian.

Wow. This is actually quite an honour. Megan **NEVER** normally lets anyone sit at her table.

What should I do? She's only inviting **ME**. I look at Brian, but he just stares at the floor.

I think it's pretty **obvious** he **DOESN'T** want to be my friend any more.

"OK, Megan," I say. "Thanks."

"Ovaltina, MOVE!" Megan says when we get to her table. "Nina's sitting there."

At first, Ovaltina's face goes like this ...

... and then like THIS.

She gives me an EXTRA-DIRTY look as she switches chairs.

OW!

PULL

This is when I realize I am now Megan's

Who's SHE?

She's Megan's FIRST Best Friend!

Wow! IMPRESSIVE!

Megan starts going on about how many **views** our last video got.

One hundred and twenty THOUSAND.

Can you BELIEVE that, Bestie?

In just ONE day!

"Uh, yeah, I know, amazing," I say as
I turn to look at Brian.

oh no,
he's all
on his
OWN!

"You're very quiet, Ovaltina," Megan says.
"What did YOU think of our video?"

Mumble
mumble.

What?

I said
I DIDN'T
WATCH IT!

OKAYYYY?!

wow, that was unexpected

I don't think I've ever heard Ovaltina say anything louder than a **WHISPER** before.

SCREECH!

You're not the **ONLY ONE** doing stuff, Megan.

I have **THINGS** going on **TOO**, you know.

Or you **WOULD**, if you ever even **ASKED** me!

"**Where's she going?**" Megan says as Ovaltina walks across the canteen to Brian's table.

"I'm not sure," I say, even though I **TOTALLY** know.

At first, Megan is so **SHOCKED** that bits of food start falling out of her mouth.

Then she begins saying **MEAN** things about Ovaltina like:

"Anyway, we don't need **HER** any more," she says.

"**Yeah**," I say, trying to sound **ENTHUSIASTIC.**
I just can't stop looking at my **OLD**
Best Friend's table.

This is the first day of me and Megan being **OFFICIAL FIRST BEST FRIENDS** and also of me **NOT** being Brian's friend **AT ALL**.

BRAND-NEW BESTIES

BESTIE FROM ANCIENT HISTORY

It's also a **NO UNIFORM** day.

I got this message from Megan last night:

Megan: Hey, Bestie! Looking forward to our first proper day as TOTAL BESTIES! 😄♥✨

Make sure you wear your love-heart tee and of course your FABULOUS TIARA! 👑✨👄

Hugs from your bestie. 😙😙

Me: Um ... was just gonna wear my hoodie to be honest.

Megan:

Uh-oh.
Exploding brain
AND screaming
face emoji! ➡️

But, Bestie, as your Bestie, I think the hoodie would be a BAD IDEA – just being honest.

Me:

Why?

Megan:

What's the point of even HAVING a Bestie if you're just gonna dress DIFFERENT?

Me:

•••

Megan:

Well?

Me:

That makes sense.

Mum is **ALL SURPRISED** when she sees me at breakfast this morning:

I explain about me and Megan being Official Best Friends now. **"What? The girl you DON'T LIKE who's always REALLY MEAN to you?"**

At first it feels weird to be wearing a tiara while everyone else **(except Megan)** is in **NORMAL** clothes.

But then people keep saying things like:

You guys are so AWESOME!

Cool TIARAS!

I wish I HAD a TIARA.

I even start to get used to it.

Nina, you look AMAZING!

I KNOW.

Then I spot Ovaltina.

she never usually wears a HOODIE

She kind of looks like she feels **SORRY** for me.

Meanwhile, Megan looks her up and down and says:

Gone back to your USUAL BORING self, I see, Ovaltina.

That didn't take long.

When I get to my desk, Brian says: "**Nina?**"
"**Yes?**"

Sorry, for a second I thought it was MEGAN.

Ever since we've become Official First Best Friends, Megan's **BOSSINESS LEVELS** have gone to the *MAXIMUM SETTING.*

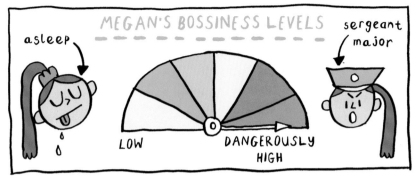

Not only is she telling me what to wear all the time, but now she's controlling every little move I make in our rehearsals for the talent show **(which is only a few days away!)**. Things like:

It's time I remind her about ...

"Unfortunately, there's **MORE** to winning than simple **CREATIVE VISION**," Megan's dad says.

"**But what it doesn't take,**" he says, "*is* **POTATOES.**" We go back to doing everything Megan's way for the rest of the rehearsal. As usual, as soon as it starts to get dark, she says she has to go and feed Lorenzo. "**Back in a sec!**"

I say, "**OK,**" like I don't care, except this time I have a **PLAN.** As soon as Megan's gone, I sneak down the hallway and into the kitchen, where I watch her go into the garden shed.

strange place to keep a **PONY**

Then I run across the garden on **TIPPY-TOES** like a

PROFESSIONAL BURGLAR

and **PEEP** in the window.

All I see is Megan filming something **small**.

But where's Lorenzo?

I check round the back of the shed, but nope, no pony there either.

— PONY-LESS

That's when I turn round and see...

I zoom in with my EYEBALL.

207

I run back round into the shed.

she has a
FAN and everything

"Megan, what's going on?" I ask.

For a
second, she
says nothing:

...

Then:

You
wouldn't
UNDERSTAND!

"If you MUST know, it's because of the GIRLS at my last school."

POSHINGTON ACADEMY for YOUNG LADIES

"They ALL had ponies, and guess what. I didn't."

WATCH OUT!

SPLAT

"It wouldn't have been so bad if the head teacher hadn't MADE me go to RIDING LESSONS."

"She'd make me RUN round the field, shouting things at me like:

"She even made me jump the FENCES."

"The other girls thought it was HILARIOUS and always called me names."

"It's the reason I ended up leaving."

"Are you going to **TELL** everyone?" she asks.
I think about it for a second and then I say:

No.

Oh, thank you, Nina! You're the **BEST** Bestie EVER!

"But there is one thing you can do for me," I say.
"Yes, **ANYTHING**," she says.
"Just name it, Bestie!"
"Put Mr Wrinkly Potato Face in the act."

"Absolutely ..."

... NO WAY!

"Are you serious?!" I say.
"After me being such a GOOD BESTIE?"
"I'm sorry, Nina, but you heard my dad."

"Hey, I'M the FAMOUS one, REMEMBER?" I say.

"I'm saying I don't need you any more. I can be
INTERNET-FAMOUS all by myself!"

Does this mean you're QUITTING the ACT?

No, because I'd get into TROUBLE with Mr Hairyson. And my MUM.

But from now on, I'll be doing ALL my videos BY MYSELF.

And you won't get ANY MORE new followers because of ME.

"You'll regret this," Megan says.

I don't think so.

Bye, Lorenzo. NICE HAIR, by the way!

THIS IS GOING TO BE SO GREAT!

At last, I am free to be

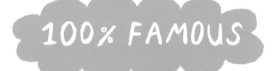

100% FAMOUS

all **BY MYSELF**.

At lunchtime, everyone in the canteen is pointing and laughing at me. The video **MUST** be about me. And it must be **BAD.** What could it be?

There's **NO WAY** I can sit in here on my own.

Back home, I log into BoogleToob straight away.

She's totally making **FUN** of me. I thought Jools was
one of my superfans! I can hardly watch.

Back on Megan's channel, there are tons of comments.
They're all **TERRIBLE.**

At least I still have all my
OWN FANS to turn to.

AMAZING AND NON-STUPID
VIDEOS BY NINA PEANUT

Subscribers: 4 !!!!!

GASP!

Only 4 fans left.

Nan   Ovaltina   Pamela

and

Brian

That's it.

... we're **FINISHED!**
New rule: no internet ever again!

NEXT MORNING

This is what I would have worn to school today if **PAPER BAGS** with **EYEHOLES** were allowed. But unfortunately they're not, so now everyone gets to point and laugh at my **ACTUAL FACE.**

Here we go.

Ha ha ha!

Wait, WHO are they laughing at?

MEGAN?!

ha! ha! ha! ha! ha!

Did she do a really bad **Sparkle Dance** too?

At lunch, I head straight for the toilets. Even though everyone's laughing at Megan now, I still have **NO ONE** to sit with in the canteen.

BRIAN AND OVALTINA: too busy being **IN LOVE**, and anyway, we're **STILL NOT SPEAKING!**

POINTY-OUT PAMELA: would just keep pointing out how **BAD** my Sparkle Dance was

It was TERRIBLE.

No, it's back to my **NEW FAVOURITE PLACE.**

SLURRP

It **STINKS** in here.

"As if **YOU** weren't the one who **TOLD** her he was just a **TOY**," Megan says. "And now she's posted a video making fun of me for **EVERYONE** to see!" (Oh, REALLY?)

It's not a very **NICE FEELING**, is it, Megan?

looks like she feels a **TINY BIT** bad

Then:

So you **ADMIT** that you were the one who **TOLD** her?

No. I didn't. But I **WISH** I had ...

"... because it was a **GENIUS IDEA!**"

HUMPH!

SNORT!

extra speed

Yikes, me and Megan have to do our **ACT** together **TOMORROW NIGHT!**

BACK HOME

The truth is, the only person I'd ever have told about Megan's fake pony would have been Brian, because we used to tell each other **EVERYTHING.**

But now we don't because he's **Ovaltina's** Best Friend, and **NOT** mine.

Nina, what's THIS?

oh no, the SPARKLES!

"I nearly tipped a bowl of old Blunky Chunks on top of them," Nan says.

"Why were they in the BIN?"

I break my "No Internet Ever Again" rule (didn't take long) and show Nan Really Cool Jools's video.

What's this very UNPLEASANT GIRL'S video got to do with your LOVELY COSTUME?

I'm TERRIBLE at dancing, Nan!

"I didn't realize it until everyone on the internet told me, but now I can never, EVER dance again," I say.

ESPECIALLY not in SPARKLES.

"Nina, I know some people — like your auntie Sheila, for example," Nan says, rolling her eyes, "think I'm not the world's GREATEST PAINTER, but that's not going to stop me painting. You know why?"

"But also because I ENJOY doing it," she says.
"Nan, that's OK for you," I say.

"So you won't ever do anything unless you can do it PERFECTLY?" Nan asks. "Exactly," I say.
"That's a shame, pumpkin," she says.

Then you'll NEVER do very much at all.

Nan leaves the sparkles on my desk and then heads back to her painting with a **Big Sigh.**

Seeing as I've **ALREADY** broken my "No Internet" rule **ONCE** today, I may as well break it **AGAIN.**

232

There are loads of horrible comments, just like I got.

What a FAKER!

I'm UNFOLLOWING her right away!

Giddy up, PHONY GIRL!!!

Part of me feels like Megan **DESERVES** this after being so **MEAN** and **BOSSY** to me. But part of me feels **BAD** for her too, because I know this must be her **WORST NIGHTMARE.** I'm **CONFUSED.**

DIAGRAM OF MY CONFUSED FEELINGS ABOUT MEGAN:

ANNOYED

FEELS BAD

up to my NECK

just past my KNEES

Result: **MOSTLY ANNOYED.**

THE TALENT SHOW WITH A TWIST!

The show *is* starting in fifteen minutes. Me and Megan hardly look at each other.

Backstage

Hi.

Hi.

uncomfortable

uncomfortable

asleep

"I know it wasn't you who told Really Cool Jools about Lorenzo, by the way," she says.
"Oh?" I say.

Yeah, it was a girl from my OLD SCHOOL.

I SHOULD'VE known.

"And I'm sorry for posting that video of you. It was really mean of me," she says.

"And I walked out because I was angry at YOU for not letting me have the POTATOES in our act," I say.

"I know," she says, "but you understand it's for the BEST, don't you?"

If we want to win, we have to STICK to THE PLAN.

annoyed levels: TOP OF HEAD

Next thing, Megan's dad comes jogging in, and says he's here to give us a **MOTIVATIONAL SPEECH.** I say: "**No, thanks. I have to get changed.**" (Just an excuse.)

sweat

Remember, we're IN IT...

...to WIN IT!!!

WOOF! WOOF!

While they're doing that, I take a look around.

Brian and Ovaltina are sitting in the corner.

Squidge

Ovaltina's dog, Daphne

They look **NERVOUS.**

All the other kids are running around doing last-minute rehearsals. Jamelia's lizard is meant to **BLINK** every time Sikandar plays **B FLAT** on his recorder.

B FLAT

While Mr Hairyson isn't looking, I sneak a peek at the audience through a hole in the curtain.

Everyone is here.

who's Anni?

why?

Dad Alfie Petulia

Uncle Freddie Doughnut Declan Auntie Sheila Nan Mum

Time for a **QUICK CHANGE.**

Yep, I kept the **SPARKLES!**

Megan thinks I'm doing it for HER

she almost calls me "BESTIE"

The curtains go back and Mr Hairyson says, "**Greetings, everyone,**" and that there's **FREE TOILET PAPER** at the back ...

... in case of any **PET MALFUNCTIONS.**

toilet accidents

It's time for the first act, which is Noel and Amber with their **Dancing Unicorn Twins.**

just DOGS in disguise →

also **NOT** → twins

While that's going on, Megan tries to hand me the **FISHING ROD.**

She looks confused, but just says, **"OK?"**

The audience starts to clap, which means me and Megan are **UP NEXT.**

Megan looks **SUPER WORRIED,** but it's **TOO LATE** for her to say anything because Mr Hairyson has just called our names. **(GULP.)**

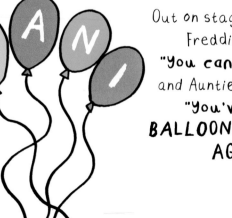

Out on stage, I hear Uncle Freddie shouting: **"You can do it, Nani!"** and Auntie Sheila saying: **"You've got the BALLOONS all mixed up AGAIN!"**

The music starts and straight away Megan and Princess are into their hoop routine.

The audience are all going **"WOO!"**
Meanwhile, I take the following from my bag:

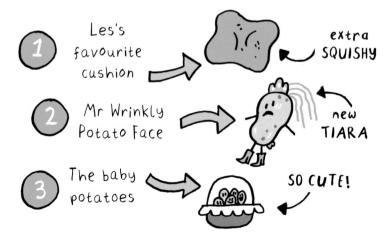

1. Les's favourite cushion → extra SQUISHY

2. Mr Wrinkly Potato Face → new TIARA

3. The baby potatoes → SO CUTE!

Then I get the baby potatoes ready for **SLEEP.**

SWEET dreams.

BOUNCE

BOING

Mr Wrinkly Potato Face is their SUPERVISOR.

Next thing I hear is Megan saying:

What are you DOING?

← hissy sound

But I just **IGNORE** her and **ADD** Les to the cushion.

Now for the **MOMENT** of **TRUTH**.

At first, Les just **stays awake.**

The audience goes **WILD.**
I KNEW this was a good trick.

Hey, where are all those roses coming from?

FLING

Huh?!
I never knew
Megan had a
CLOWN BIKE!

still

SNORE!

This is just **showing off** if you ask me.

Way to go,
CHAMP!

It's time to move on to the **NEXT PHASE** of my act.

That's right!

It's my SPARKLE DANCE.

HOP

It's going pretty well, except for the **VOICES IN MY HEAD.**

She should have stuck to FISHING RODS!

She looks like a WOBBLY PENGUIN!

Then in Real Life, Megan says:

Stop this NOW. You're RUINING MY CHANCES!

For **REVENGE,** I dance even **HARDER.**

SWEAT

ponytail
all
WAGGLY

legs and arms
gone EXTRA
WOBBLY
(didn't know
they could DO
that)

That's when I **BUMP** into Megan
(who's still on her clown bike).

Agh!

WHOOPS!

Somehow ...

... we end up ...

... like **THIS**.

The audience goes **EVEN WILDER** this time.
Nan and Mum stand up to clap.

Mr Hairyson gives
us his **angry**
**"GET OFF
THE STAGE!"**
face because we've
gone way over time.

Backstage, loads of people are saying,
"Wow, that was an AMAZING ENDING! you
two must have practised that for AGES!"

We made
a PRETTY
GOOD TEAM
in the end,
didn't we?

just about

Brian and Ovaltina are up next.

First, Ovaltina walks on stage with Daphne. They sit at the piano and start to play a **FANCY TUNE** from the **OLDEN DAYS.**

can play with her **PAWS**, which is QUITE **TALENTED** (for a **DOG**)

Then Brian comes on carrying Squidge under one arm and pulling a whole town made from **CEREAL BOXES** with the other.

SQUIDGE TOWN

↑ toilet-roll tubes

↖ also - WOW

He puts Squidge down and starts to read from a piece of paper.

SQUIDGE TOWN

This is Squidge. He is having a NORMAL DAY in Squidge Town.

A SCIENCE BOOK

cardboard

"Look, he's reading a book." Brian dangles the TINIEST book I've ever seen into Squidge's cage.

Squidge nibbles the edge of it.

"Now he's phoning his nan."

also
cardboard

"They talk about the weather and what
they are going to have for lunch.

Oh no! Squidge
is out of
CUCUMBER
SLICES!"

Aaaaooooo!

Daphne does a little
howl to show the
SERIOUSNESS of
the situation.

"Look in the
fridge
again, Squidge,"
Brian says.

"What's that behind the CARROTS?"

cardboard fridge

SNIFF!

"It's CUCUMBER SLICES!"

This time, Brian has **REAL** cucumber slices he took out of his lunch box.

CHOMP

CHEW

80

We all watch while Squidge eats them **LIVE ON STAGE.**

Ovaltina and Daphne play a **HAPPY TUNE.**

Then Brian says: **"The end."**

The whole audience stands up to cheer. Ovaltina's mother has tears in her eyes, and Brian's dad is clapping his hands above his head.

That's when I realize that Brian's **IDEA** was

AMAZING!

By the end of the show, there are only a **few** rolls of toilet roll left.

We are all sitting out in the front now, and Mr Hairyson comes on stage to announce the **TOP THREE PERFORMANCES.**

He clears his throat and says:
"In **THIRD** place we have Megan Dunne and Nina Peanut with their **HOOP EXTRAVAGANZA!**"
Everyone claps.

This is Megan's face.

And this is **MY** face when I turn round and Nan says, "I'm so proud of you, **PUMPKIN!**"

Second place goes to Jamelia Habibi and Sikander Sharma. Megan's dad jumps up and says:
"**WHAT? Beaten by a BLINKING LIZARD? This competition's a JOKE!**"

insulted

After Mr Dunne is asked to "**Please sit down**", Mr Hairyson announces the winners.

"Brian Babalola and Ovaltina Lemington for their MOVING performance of a NORMAL DAY IN THE LIFE OF A HAMSTER."

This one's for YOU, Squidge!

Seeing Brian up there on stage is making me wonder how come I never realized he's a **CREATIVE GENIUS** too?

Maybe he's right — maybe I **DIDN'T** ever listen to him? Is that why we always ended up doing **MY** genius ideas and not **his?**

UH-OH, DOES THIS MEAN ...

... I'm a

BIG MEAN
BOSSY-PANTS

like MEGAN?!

This is the
SCARIEST
THOUGHT I'VE
EVER HAD!

even scarier
than this

After the show, I go to find Brian. He's waggling his trophy in front of his brother Jason's face.

"Ahem," I say.

"Oh," Brian says.

"I'm sorry."

"Oh," he says again.

WAGGLE

"You were right. I DON'T listen," I say.

And Squidge Town WAS an AMAZING idea.

Oh.

↑
THIRD time!

After a second:

Will you and Ovaltina be getting MARRIED soon?

What?! Don't say THAT!

"She's just a FRIEND!" he says.

In fact, I'd really like it if ALL THREE of us could be FRIENDS?

Does this mean Ovaltina is Brian's **FIRST** Best Friend, and I'm only his **SECOND?** Now is probably not the best time for this question.

Then Ovaltina comes running over.
"Congratulations," I say.

↑ I actually really mean it

Then Ovaltina says, **"Guys, I kind of FEEL BAD for Megan."** My "Feeling Bad for Megan" levels are down in my **ANKLES.**

"I know she can be a **REAL PAIN**," Ovaltina says, "but she has her good points too."

Like WHAT?

"You probably don't remember, but I didn't have any friends until Megan started here," Ovaltina says. "She was the first one to play with me and invite me to her house."

I know what it feels like to be ALL ALONE.

"I really think we should give her a **CHANCE**," Ovaltina says.

Me and Brian look at each other like that's **NOT** such a great idea.

But it's too late. Ovaltina's **already** gone to talk to her, and **two seconds** later ...

Hi!!

Isn't this NICE? ALL of us hanging out TOGETHER!

Next thing, Pointy-Out Pamela comes over.

I'm a RABBIT-CHICKEN. If I had a pet it would be THIS.

of course

You guys are all BEST FRIENDS now.

uh, not quite

"I think your act could've used a little more ... OOMPH."

You know, like a HOOP TRICK, or something?

Uh, Megan? We have to GO HOME now.

Phew. "Oh, right," Megan says, sounding a bit surprised.

See you after half-term.

Should be **interesting.**

When it's finally just me and Brian, I say, "**Want to come over to mine this Saturday?**"

We can eat BRAIN FOOD and come up with CREATIVE GENIUS IDEAS for stuff. Just like in the good old days.

why does he have a PAINED look on his face?

It's just I'm meant to be going to Ovaltina's for CHURROS that day.

again?!

I KNEW I wasn't his First Best Friend any more.

Oh, OK.

"But you should come!" he says. "I know Ovaltina will want you to."

You're going to LOVE churros!

we'll see

drooling already

IN CASE YOU'RE WONDERING ...

... **I UN-DELETED** my video channel.
But now instead of doing **BORING CAT** videos
just because they get loads of likes ...

LOOK! CAT LICKING SHOE! CUTE!!

17k LIKES!

... I've gone back to doing **CREATIVE GENIUS** videos like this one:

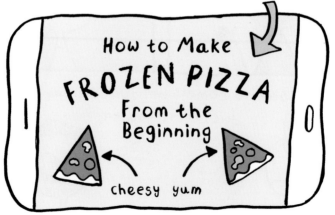

How to Make
FROZEN PIZZA
From the Beginning

cheesy yum

First, get one from the FREEZER.

Next, TAKE IT OUT of the box.

Get an ADULT to do the OVEN BIT.

265

Acknowledgements

Thank you first and foremost to my agent, Lydia Silver, for her energy and support, for being the first one to say 'Yes!' and for finding a brilliant home for Nina Peanut.

Huge thanks also to my editor Lauren Fortune, for her excellent guidance, good humour and inordinate love of cats.

Finally, a big thank you to all the unseen hands that worked so hard to help bring this book to fruition.